The Sorceress

Direction artistique : Jamie Keenan
Mise en page : JOUVE Saran

Enregistrements, montage et mixage : Studio Corby
Texte lu par Karin Morgan

 - ISBN 978-2-278-07228-6 - Imprimé en France
Dépôt légal : 7228/01
Achevé d'imprimer par EMD S.A.S. en avril 2012 - N° 26445

The Sorceress

Philippa
Boston

didier

AN HISTORICAL NOTE

This story takes place in the year 1583. England at this time was under the reign of Elizabeth I – 'Queen Bess' – whose mother, Anne Boleyn, had been executed as a sorceress (or witch) when Elizabeth was still an infant.

The English laws on sorcery under Elizabeth I were less severe than those in continental Europe at the time. Because England had broken with the Catholic Church under the reign of Elizabeth's father, Henry VIII, sorcery was not considered to be heresy. Contrary to Catholic practise at the time, a distinction was made in England between 'black witches', who practised secret arts to do harm to others, and 'white witches' or 'wise women', who had a knowledge of the medicinal properties of plants.

Under Elizabeth's reign, there were 270 trials for sorcery in total. The majority of these took place in Essex, a county in south-east England where there were regular outbreaks of hysteria on the subject in a town called Chelmsford. One such trial of fourteen witches took place in 1582, the year before this story happens.

Chapter 1

I

THE CLEAR AUGUST SKY OVER OXFORD was darkening rapidly as Maude Mansfield exited Christ Church College. Although she was not a timid girl, the first thunder-clap of the storm made her jump as she emerged from the college on to the crowded city street.

To her left the South Gate was busier than usual. People outside the city walls had seen the storm approaching across the fields and were moving fast to take refuge. Carts, animals and humans pushed and jostled to get through the gate.

Maude had not realised there was a storm coming. The day had been hot and humid, as had every day for weeks now. Some of the older people said 1583 was the hottest summer since a Queen sat on the throne. It was an intense heat that turned the milk and made the meat go bad. The townspeople sweated, and the city stank of excrement and decomposing rubbish.

By the time Maude reached Brewer Street the first fat drops of rain began to fall. She pulled her cloak further over her head and around her body, cursing her elder sister under her breath.

"Jane has another colic! God's teeth! I am glad not to be such a fragile damsel of a female as she! Huh! And yet I have to play the damsel's servant girl." She hurried on her way towards the house of Susan O'Flaherty, the woman who sold healing potions.

The rain gave up all reserve and fell now in thundering sheets. The damp smell of fermentation from the beer brewery filled Maude's nostrils as she ran towards the corner.

Although not a 'fragile damsel' like her sister, Maude cried out in shock as even louder lightning ripped across the sky, and she bumped straight in to a similarly-hooded figure rushing the other way. They both cried out in surprise.

"My apologies!" shouted Maude, over the noise of the storm.

"No mine, indeed, ma'am!"

"Susan?" Maude said, seeing it was the potion-seller herself.

"Mistress Mansfield? 'Tis you! Why in God's name are you out in this storm?"

"I am going to your house, Susan, for a potion for Jane!" Maude said, pulling Susan O'Flaherty out of the rain to shelter under an ornate doorway. "And surely I could ask you the same question? Why are *you* out in this?"

"Oh Mistress Mansfield, I cannot stop! A lady staying at the Flying Horse Tavern has called for me – she's terrible sick and needs my help, the messenger said. But… oh Lord, Mistress Mansfield! I was instructed to tell no one and here I am telling you!" Susan put her hand to her mouth, "You must forget – I never said nothing, d'you see? Why she wants *me*, I don't know. It's not the likes of me that gets called to smart taverns like the Flying Horse, but an apothecary."

"But you are the best potion-maker in the whole of Oxford, Susan!" Maude protested, "That's why I was on my way to see you – to get an infusion for Jane. It's her colic – again! I will walk with you and take your advice, if I may."

The two women hurried back along Brewer Street towards the centre of the city, bent against the driving rain.

"Tell her to drink an infusion of the chamomile I gave you for now," Susan O'Flaherty said as they walked, "If you come to my house tomorrow morning I'll give you some other herbs that will help. And remember – place warm stones on the muscles. Now if you will excuse me, Mistress, the man was most insistent I hurry. God bless you and keep you dry, Mistress."

"God bless you too, Susan! 'Til tomorrow then, in the morning."

II

"What do you mean 'she's gone,' Patrick?" asked Maude, looking down at Susan O'Flaherty's little boy the next morning. "She told me especially to come at this time."

"She said she might be gone an hour or two, Mistress Mansfield," said the young boy, frowning against the bright morning sun, "but she has been out all night and not sent word to us."

"But that's not like her, Patrick. Not a word, nothing?"

"Nothing, Mistress," the boy confirmed unhappily, "I went to the Flying Horse Inn to ask after her and they sent me away most nastily. They called mother a sorceress and said they wouldn't allow the likes of her past the door. And they hit me, Mistress, hit me so hard my ear is still smarting from the blow."

"The monsters!" said Maude, rubbing the poor boy's ear. "I know she was there. She was specially asked for – she told me."

"It's true, Mistress, we all heard the man ask for her – urgent like – didn't we?"

The other two, even smaller children nodded vigorously at Maude, their neat, little brows furrowed with concern.

"'Flying Horse Inn' he said, clear as day. And then the storm, and she ain't come back..."

Tears welled up in the eyes of the brave little boy, fists clenched at his sides as he struggled to keep control of his fears.

Maude hugged him to her and the other two instantly fell upon her skirts too. She glanced desperately around the room as the three children cried, hoping to see some explanation. But there was nothing to help her except silent bottles of herbs and potions.

III

Out on the street Maude lifted her face to the sun. The storm had cleared the air. She headed uphill, away from the marshy streets and re-entered the city through the breach in the city walls between the west and little gates. She walked east along Great Bailey, towards the great carre-forks at St Martin's Church.

Deep in thought about Susan and wondering why she had not come home, Maude jumped as she heard,

"Penny for your thoughts, pretty lady!" close to her ear.

She looked up in to the face of a smiling, handsome young man in a smart green doublet.

"Oh Harry!" she smiled to see her favourite Oxford scholar at her side. "I was miles away – I didn't see you."

"I could see that," said Harry Hopetoun, turning to walk along Great Bailey with her. "So – what about those thoughts? I meant what I said, Mistress Mansfield, I'd give a penny to know what you were thinking. You looked as if you were wrestling with an interesting problem?"

Maude pursed her lips and frowned a little. Harry's expression softened at this familiar expression of hers, for he was as fond of Maude Mansfield as she was fond of him, although he was better at hiding it.

"A strange business, Sir Harry. Worth more than a mere penny, I think. Maybe nothing to worry about. You remember the woman Susan O'Flaherty?"

"The potion-making woman?"

"Yes, the one who helped us clear John de Courcy's good name last Yuletide, when he was so falsely accused*?"

Maude recounted her meeting of the night before and Susan's strange disappearance.

"Maybe it was another tavern," Harry suggested. "Maybe she has gone straight to another sick person."

"That's a lot of maybes, Sir Harry."

"Supposition, Mistress, is an integral part of the legal process."

"And like so many things, Sir Harry, you take it too far. So you will not help me?"

Harry looked at Maude's expression and realised she was genuinely worried.

"Of course I will help you. I will always help you." He bowed before her. "Permit me to make some enquiries about town and we will no doubt discover what has happened to Susan O'Flaherty. But please... can't we go back to calling each other 'Harry' and 'Maude', like we used to?"

* See *The Fortunes of John de Courcy* by Philippa Boston in the Paper Planes collection.

Maude cuffed Harry gently on the arm.

"No, Sir Harry. I have told you. Father has been most stern with me – now we are older, we must address each other properly. Otherwise people might think that we have an improper friendship."

Harry tried to compose his face and suppress a smile as he accompanied the pretty girl on through the crowds.

Chapter 2

I

"SUSAN O'FLAHERTY IS LOCKED IN BOCARDO, Maude," Harry informed her the next morning, he and his friend John de Courcy having made enquiries about town.

"Bocardo?" Maude frowned, "But why? No one is locked in Bocardo anymore unless they must be quarantined?"

"She is accused of witchcraft, so they say," he explained. "And is confined in Bocardo away from other souls so she cannot use her satanic powers on them. They say only the presence of a Bishop can guarantee people will be safe from her."

"But who accuses her?" Maude asked in horror.

"The Reverend Stoneworthy, who preaches out of St Clement's Church."

"That black-feathered, humourless fellow that shouts about sin in the Corn Market?"

"The same," Harry confirmed. "He is her main accuser, and he has witnesses, of course, townspeople suspicious of poor Susan."

"I knew it! Didn't I say, Harry?"

"You did."

"And I was right!"

"You were."

Maude was so fired up with excitement and indignation that she was unaware of the effect she was having on the young man. Striding to and fro in her well-cut morning gown, her undressed, chaotic curls tumbling down her back and the flush in her cheek made Harry quite forget why he was there.

"We must talk to her, Harry."

"To who?"

"To *Susan*, you goose. Who did you think: Queen Bess?"

"We cannot. She is locked up all alone and none may go near her. They say her witchery has made her mad and ill with a sweating sickness – she rants about the plague."

"What tosh! She has caught a cold in the storm, that is all, as any woman would who gives all her food to her children and then gets soaking wet. I'd bet my life on it. I will find a way to see her, Harry."

"But what if it is the pestilence?"

"You may stay with the guard creating a distraction. I will see the situation with Susan."

"And did you talk to the people at the Flying Horse Tavern?"

"Of course – I have not told you! The tavern keeper is willing to swear on the great Bible that there was no one sick in the tavern that night."

"He said that?"

"To me, yesterday. Nobody with any sickness at the tavern since last Spring's ague. No knowledge of Susan being there either. I could not speak long with him as he was travelling on his cart and was in a hurry. But he said he would swear on the great bible."

"Which is worth nothing if he is a closet papist," added Harry cynically.

"He did not seem the type."

"What is he like, this tavern keeper?"

"He is a charming man, most polite. He was very apologetic that he did not have the time to speak to me, and invited me, with such a very friendly smile, to return to take a mug of something and talk more if I wished. And he is an Associate of the Mayor too – at such a young age..."

Harry noticed that Maude was blushing slightly and fixed her with a hard stare.

"What do you mean 'young age'?"

"Well he can't be more than thirty years of age..."

"That *old*?"

"It's not *that* old."

The door opened and Jane Mansfield entered, halted when she saw Harry in the room and instinctively raised a hand to check her hair. She smiled up at him through her eyelashes.

"Why, Sir Harry, you are come so early to visit?" She smiled her most winning smile at the handsome legal scholar.

"Good morning, Miss Mansfield," said Harry with a bow. "Yes, I am come to inform your sister of the location of the apothecary..."

"You have found her finally? There, Maude – didn't I tell you she would come back?" Jane smiled triumphantly at her sister.

"Not exactly, Miss Mansfield. My friend John de Courcy made enquiries on her behalf and discovered she is held in Bocardo."

"Mr de Courcy?" gasped Jane, indifferent to the news that Mrs O'Flaherty was in gaol. "Why would such an important man as Mr de Courcy be making enquiries about that woman?"

"Because she helped prove his innocence when we all believed him innocent and the rest of the world did not? Do you remember, sister? And 'that woman', as you call her, testified on his behalf, even at great personal risk to herself and her children?"

Jane blushed at the memory of her own lack of belief in John de Courcy's innocence and her willingness to listen to the venomous lies of his enemies.

"Of course, I remember. It is kind of him to give his time to the woman, even so."

"I suppose my friend John feels that he must repay the favour. He is that sort of a man, Miss Mansfield: full of integrity."

Jane frowned slightly, unsure whether Harry too was making fun of her or not.

II

Maude, swathed in her dark cloak, too hot for the end of summer, but necessary to preserve her identity, emerged from the door that led from the back of the Master's lodgings on to the lane at the south side of Christ Church College.

She made her way up South Street and battled with the carts and people fighting their way through the carre-forks, and on down the Corn Market towards the North Gate.

She spotted Harry and John waiting as planned, by the New Inn. As she approached Harry was telling John about their teasing of Jane.

"Poor Jane!" said Maude. "She looked as though she had swallowed an artichoke! We must stop persecuting her on Mr de Courcy's behalf, Sir Harry."

"Indeed you must!" said John, a little too vehemently. Maude and Harry turned curious expressions on him.

"*Must* we, Mr de Courcy? And why might that be? I thought that now you were courted by so many smart maids of Oxford, you no longer thought of my sister?"

"Indeed, Miss Mansfield, I am *not* courted, indeed I am *not*, by anyone – who are these maids you speak of? And your sister – well, of course I think – I mean... why, I don't know what – I am surprised that – well, I don't believe in making fun of people..."

Maude and Harry laughed at John's stammering embarrassment. Harry clapped a hand on his friend's shoulder.

"Now don't you worry, Johnny, we are only making fun of you too. You think about whatever or whomever you want to think about. Now – to the job in hand."

"Are you decided on your part, Mr de Courcy?" asked Maude.

John nodded and gestured to a man along the street from them, waiting with a basket of bread.

"I will be ready to distract the gaoler when the time comes, Mistress Maude," he said.

"Good luck! I'll be as quick as I can. Sir Harry – lead on to hell on earth!"

III

The guard snorted, waking from his sleep and lifting his head as Harry approached him.

"Eh? What? Who?" he grunted, shuffling to his feet and rubbing his red, bulbous nose.

"A cooler morning since the rains, guard, wouldn't you say?" Harry said, moving past the guard to look out the window at the street below.

"I would, sir, but tell me your business here." The guard squinted at Harry, then at the window.

"I hear you have a certain goodwife here, guard, Susan O'Flaherty?"

"The witch? Aye, she's here. But no 'good' goes with her and none may speak to her or go near her."

"No witch also, I believe," Harry said. "Simply a wise woman with a gift for healing. I'm sure you have heard this of her?"

The guard looked to left and right even though the room was empty and leant in towards Harry. Harry felt his stomach turn at the odour coming from the man's rotting mouth.

"Why I have, sir," the guard whispered. "She came to my own wife, Sarah, when she had a sore on her leg that had plagued her for months, sir, all filled with puss and …."

Harry held up his hand to stop the man right there.

"As I said, she is no witch. But how is it then you hold her here?"

"Not I, sir, I am simply the guard. It is *them*. She is accused of witchery, plain as day, by the Reverend Stoneworthy, as speaks out of St Clement's Church. He says she has cast spells on his horses and fouled his dairy, and has witnesses to say other acts of witchery too."

"His *horses*, you say?"

There was a noise in the street outside.

"What goes in the street below, guard? Do you hear?"

The guard moved eagerly towards the window to look down upon the North Gate, always a lively spot. Below, a young gentleman scholar – none other than John de Courcy – had collided with a baker carrying a tray. Bread was rolling in the street and an entertaining scene held the attention of all around.

As the two men watched from the window, a dark-cloaked figure moved swiftly across the room behind them toward the cells.

IV

Maude stood with a handkerchief over her nose to help with the stink that came from the cells.

"Susan!"

"Eh?"

"Ssh! Susan! It is I, Maude Mansfield! Can you speak with me?"

A face appeared a way back from the iron grille in the door of the cell to Maude's right.

"Oh my lady! 'Tis you. Do not come near me. I fear I am diseased, Mistress."

"With the plague, you mean? But why would you have the plague?"

"I cannot say, Mistress! I cannot! But I fear it is true. I fear so many things. They threatened me so. There is a sweating upon me. A fever."

"A fever is not the plague. You know that." Maude's eyes were becoming accustomed to the half light of the passage. "Oh my Lord! Your face, Susan! What have they done to you?"

The poor, dishevelled figure on the other side of the grille touched her fingers to her face and winced in pain as she did so.

"Tell me, Susan, all that happened. Why are you here? Some say witchery – is it true that you are accused?"

"Aye Mistress, it is true that I am accused, but it is not the truth, Lady, you know..."

"Ssh, of course I know. And I am here to help you. But you must tell me..."

"But no one is allowed near me – how are you come?"

"No time for that. Enough that I am here. What happened after we met in the storm?"

"I cannot say, Mistress. They have said they will kill my children if I do. I dare not. I cannot.

They say they'll burn my babies in their beds..." Susan stopped talking and disappeared from view.

"Ssh, Susan. Do not upset yourself. Your children will not be harmed if we can help it. But you must tell me what happened. Did you reach the Flying Horse after we parted?"

"I did, Mistress, although I now wish I had not."

"They deny you were ever there."

"Oh I was there."

"And the sick person?"

"The poor lady with the Virgin's mark."

"The what?"

"Where the Virgin Mary strokes a person's head, their hair turns white – a streak of white in the darkest hair. I am afraid I am diseased by her."

"How is she?"

"I have already said too much. I have put my children in danger."

"But you must let us help you."

"They say I may not be helped – by no-one, Mistress Mansfield. That's what they said. And they will find me guilty and hang me for a witch.

But at least my soul will be pure in the eyes of God and my three young ones will be safe, God willing."

"Hell's teeth Susan! No! You cannot say that. You are not a witch. You are a good woman. I will not let these mad ministers spread such lies. Answer one thing – did you treat the woman you speak of at the Flying Horse?"

"I did. Although, Lord help me, there was little I could do for her by then. I was seized on my way home before dawn. I say no more. Stay away from me. I am not clean. I would rather die than see harm come to my children. They are so very small..."

Maude could hear the muffled sobbing through the grille.

"Here, Susan, I must go before I am discovered, take these – your own potions, they will help, and this food. Quick, before I am found out and we both suffer. Come – take it."

As Susan appeared again at the grille, Maude looked anxiously for signs of disease but there were none amongst the bruises on her face and arms.

"When you are gone from here, boil sage in strong wine, Mistress. Drink it and gargle it in your throat. It will help keep you safe. God bless you Mistress."

"And you, dear Susan."

Maude moved nimbly back down the dark corridor and ran silently behind the guard and Harry, who had his arm around the man's shoulder as they roared with laughter at something in the street below.

V

The Reverend Stoneworthy, dressed all in black, his long hair clinging to the sharp angles of his head, stood in the pulpit high above the small congregation in the church. He pushed down on his large, fat hands, shoulders hunched and glared at the anxious flock below him, like a wolf deciding which one he would eat first.

"Which of you miserable sinners will feel the flesh-burning agony of damnation?" he began. "Which of you has a conscience clear of the sins of mankind?"

Maude and Harry, in a back pew, exchanged glances of surprise.

But this was only a gentle beginning. Reverend Stoneworthy's rantings rose from this low to became stronger and louder and more graphic, until the rasping voice of the preacher and the graphically painted visions of the agonies of hell, made the congregation scared even to twitch or scratch.

"And at this time, the end of the wicked summer when wantons sully our streets with their uncovered flesh, we must be vigilant to the ways of Lucifer himself! When our own town has been touched by *sorcery*!"

Some of the congregation gasped as the word hit them like a whip. They glanced anxiously this way and that as if one of their number were about to be exposed as the witch.

"The devil is walking amongst us, but we have discovered him and will strike him down, by the grace of God..." Reverend Stoneworthy crossed himself and the congregation enthusiastically followed suit. "We will uncover each and every agent of the devil and they shall feel the heat of the Lord's anger upon their skin."

Reverend Stoneworthy was staring out from the pulpit, his eyes filled with a palpable excitement at the thought of torturing these supposed sinners. Maude felt some of her natural courage escape her in the face of this man, his face livid, his eyes wide, licking his dry lips at the thought of torturing and killing a good woman like Susan O'Flaherty who had never done any harm.

After the sermon, Maude said she would wait at a distance while Harry talked to the Reverend Stoneworthy. She stood near a big oak tree and watched the two men. Harry was his usual calm self, but the Reverend gesticulated wildly as they talked. Eventually, Harry took his leave.

"The man's as mad as a hatter, or putting on a very good show of it," he informed her. "He says Susan made his horses lame, she turned the milk sour, the butter to curdle..."

"But how did she have access to his horses or his dairy?"

"Apparently she did it all from a distance as she had a grudge against the Reverend's wife, Agnes."

"That man is married? Poor Agnes!"

"He says Agnes took some potions from Susan and they were no good, so Agnes told Susan so.

He says Agnes is not the only one – apparently he has several witnesses who will speak against Susan O'Flaherty."

"All stupid townswomen, I'll warrant, who mistrust anyone that isn't born within the city walls. Idiots! Dangerous, misguided idiots! How can they play with a good woman's life like this?"

"These are strange times, Mistress Maude. How can the simple people tell what is right and what is wrong? In the past fifty years our rulers have told us that black is white and white is black. It is difficult even for us with our books and our education to know what is true anymore. That is where this rash of witch hunting has sprung from. When truth is no longer set in learning and tradition, truth belongs to those who shout loudest, and they are often not the ones who should be listened to."

"I wish all the world were as wise as you, Harry – *Sir* Harry."

– And I wish all women were as remarkable as you, thought Harry, fighting the urge to take hold of Maude's gloved hand in his own as they walked back in to the town.

VI

Maude's father was standing in front of the fireplace, his hands behind his back, waiting for her. His normally twinkling blue eyes were almost hidden by his frown. She knew she was in trouble.

"Come in. Shut the door. Sit down."

Maude did as she was told.

"Jane tells me you have been out alone again, this very day, quite openly with Sir Harry Hopetoun and no chaperone."

"We went to church sir, and I was fully veiled – Jane said that..."

"No matter where, how and what Jane said, Mistress Maude! I see that in spite of my commands, you have carried on as if you were still twelve years old. When will you listen, tell me? You are now sixteen, Maude. You are old enough to marry and *certainly* old enough for people to talk and ruin your reputation and your chances of making a good marriage."

"But it is only Harry, sir – "

"*Sir* Harry, Maude! For pity's sake, girl! Do you not hear what I say? Do you not understand plain English any more? Your friendship with *Sir* Harry is no longer seemly."

"But one cannot discard a friendship, sir, as if it were last year's style of ruff. It is not fashion, sir, it is friendship."

This made Sir Michael Mansfield draw breath, but only for a moment.

"There is an age, Maude, at which such *friendships* either become a path to a marriage contract or are not suitable. No more, no less. You are of that age. So tell me – which way does your friendship with Harry fall?"

Maude was furious to feel herself blushing under the stern, but affectionate eye of her father as he scrutinised her. No one knew her as well as he. No one supported her as he had always done.

Because of the death of her mother, Mansfield had allowed Maude liberties of education and experience unknown to girls of her position. She did not wish to make him regret it.

"I see from the rosy glow of your cheek, Maude, that friendship is not all that you see in Sir Harry Hopetoun."

Chapter 3

I

HARRY SAT BROODING IN FRONT OF THE FIRE in his rooms. Maude's father, the Master of Christ Church, had summoned him for a severe reprimand. Why could people not see that his friendship with Maude was innocent? Harry took another gulp of the wine he held in his left hand.

A noise on the stair made him glance towards the door as his friend, John de Courcy, came into the room and dropped into a chair.

"A dreadful tale, Harry! My father sent me word that a lady of my home town of Burford, Mrs Pennyquick, has been found cruelly attacked and left dead on the high road south no more than three miles from Oxford's city gate – on the road near the Sandy Ford. Her nephew who was accompanying her has disappeared. I have known Mrs Pennyquick all my life, Harry – she is the wife of the paper merchant in Burford."

Harry looked shocked.

"But there is more," John continued. "Mrs Pennyquick was in Oxford to visit shops and procure goods before she travelled to her sister's house near Henleigh. And where do you suppose she was staying while in Oxford?"

"How would I know a thing like–"

"The Flying Horse Tavern!"

There was a silence as the two friends stared at each other.

Harry rubbed his face with his hands and exercised his face as if it could not decide which expression it should take.

"Dare I ask what night it was she stayed at the Flying Horse?"

"This Monday last."

"And she was found when?"

"At some time on Tuesday."

"Do we know who found her?"

"We do. When the horse Mrs Pennyquick had hired returned to its stable at the Flying Horse Tavern with no rider, the landlord, Horniman, went to look for her."

"How did he know where to look?"

"He knew she and her nephew had set out at dawn for Henleigh, so took this same route. He found her body, battered and robbed, to the side of the road near Sandy Ford."

Harry winced at the thought.

"And the nephew?"

"No sign. Nor any sign of his horse – perhaps he was murdered too, his body hidden and his horse stolen, but the other horse got away back to the Flying Horse."

"Can there be any connection between this woman Pennyquick and the one Susan treated who supposedly never existed, Johnny? Why should there be?"

"There is no 'should' about it, Harry. All we have is coincidence. Two women supposedly stayed at the Flying Horse Tavern on Monday night. One an anonymous sick woman who it seems was never there. No one except Susan O'Flaherty has any knowledge of her presence, and the tavern-keeper insists that Susan O'Flaherty herself did not visit the Flying Horse that night. The second woman leaves the tavern at dawn the next day with her nephew, healthy and trotting gaily on a horse, only to be attacked by unknown villains and left dead on the road. What does this tell us?"

"That it's probably best not to stay at the Flying Horse?" Harry giggled drunkenly.

"I think the rest will have to wait until morning," John said wearily. "You are obviously not in a fit condition to do anything sensible now."

"But I have to tell Maude." Harry tried to get up out of his chair but fell over.

"Harry, man, you are drunk! And anyway, I thought you were no longer allowed to tell Maude Mansfield anything that wasn't within the hearing of a chaperone."

"But I cannot keep this from her," said Harry from the floor. "It was Maude, after all, who started us on this business. She cannot be left out of it."

"She must be, Harry."

"No. Can't you see how that would offend her? She might not be allowed the freedom to live as we do, but I can still talk to her in her own house. I can still write to her and send her word of this new element in the mystery – if it is one. She sees connections where no one else does. She is useful, John."

"Merely *useful,* Harry?"

Harry picked up the nearest cushion and threw it at John, who ducked out of its way and laughed.

II

The next morning Maude stood impatiently, while Macebius, the wise old law tutor of the college, cast his eyes over Harry's letter.

"So what do you think, Macebius?" She asked anxiously.

"Why, I think young Sir Harry was intoxicated when he wrote this!"

Maude laughed. "We can all see that, sir! But you tease me, Master Macebius. I have come for your help. You can always see sense where I see none. What do you think of the letter?

Macebius shifted his heavy form and was about to speak when the door flew open.

"Mr de Courcy! And Sir Harry! Oh dear!" Maude started. Harry stared at her, not sure whether to come in or leave.

"Mr de Courcy, please shut the door, before the Master hears these two are in same room and has us all thrown out of college," said Macebius wearily.

"Sir Harry, I am so sorry for the trouble I have caused you," said Maude hurriedly. "I did not know my father was going to summon you for a verbal whipping. I do hope he was not too severe with you."

"No, no, ow!" Harry tried a half smile and winced as it hurt his head.

"I fear he drove you to find solace at the bottom of a goblet of wine, Harry?" Macebius ventured. "Did the goblet also help you write the paper I am waiting for?"

"Goblet? A barrel, more like," added John helpfully.

Harry ignored them.

"Mistress Maude, your noble father was no more vicious than old Macebius here has sometimes been about my Aristotelian arguments. But why does your father insist on seeing impropriety where there is none. We are simply friends – I do not see what the fuss is about."

"No – I mean – yes, of course, I agree with you," stuttered Maude, not normally lost for words, and she turned away towards the bookcase to replace her book so that Harry should not spy the disappointment in her face.

"Macebius we are come to ask your advice on this matter of the..."

"Yes, yes," said Macebius waving the letter at John. "Maude and I were discussing it when you burst in like a couple of knaves."

Macebius settled himself back in his wooden, throne-like chair, folded his hands across his round belly, and questioned Harry and John about the death of Mrs Pennyquick...

"So we must go to Burford!" said Maude suddenly.

"We – to Burford?" asked Macebius.

"That is where the lady lived. It says here that the lady lived in your own home town, Mr de Courcy, that you knew her. So we must go and talk to her family. We must find out if there is any connection between her death and Susan O'Flaherty's arrest for witchcraft!"

"*We* must go, Mistress Mansfield? *We* must talk to her family?"

"Yes – you and me, Sir Harry."

Harry looked amazed. "I know *I* may go, or John, or even Old Macebius if there were a horse strong enough to carry him, but *you* cannot. Have you forgotten already that your father has forbidden you to go abroad, even in the streets of this city, without your sister or another chaperone?"

"Really, Sir Harry, there is no use in you going without me. You are sure to miss some vital evidence," Maude argued. "John cannot go with me because if we were discovered he would have to marry me, and that would be most complicated to explain to my sister. So it must be you, Harry. I can dress as your clerk and so talk to the servants. I pass very well for a boy. No one will know."

Macebius laughed aloud and slapped the table.

"That'll teach you for your rude comments on my fine frame, Sir Harry!"

John shook his head and Harry looked terrified.

"Mistress Mansfield, you cannot, really you cannot!"

"Will you stop saying 'you cannot', Harry. You know it only makes me more determined when I am told I may not do something."

"But what if your identity is exposed? And how do you suppose to hide your absence – for days – from your father and sister?"

"I will hide nothing. My father has been threatening to send me to Aunt Catherine in Lechlade for weeks now. He says I will be one less trouble for him and away from the city if the Venetian plague travels east from Bristol. Well, Aunt Catherine will fall ill – not seriously – and need her niece to nurse her for a day or two. And Burford is close to Lechlade, after all, so it is barely a falsehood."

"But what if your disguise does not hold and you are exposed, as I said?" demanded Harry.

"We have been through this before, Sir Harry. You would have to marry me to save my reputation. Believe me, it is not a resolution that I desire any more than you – I do not think I would be any good at obeying my husband."

Macebius echoed a heartfelt "Nor do I! But it would make a comic show!"

"Mistress Mansfield I..."

"Oh Harry, please recover your humour. You have become so serious now you are almost twenty!" Maude laughed, "I am happy to risk all. You risk nothing."

"But, but..."

"But nothing. All you need to do is to meet me at the New Inn as soon as you are able, with two good horses ready."

Chapter 4

I

"WHAT DO YOU THINK, SIR HARRY? Will I pass with the good folk of Burford?" asked Maude as they cantered west from Oxford, towards Witney.

"What I think is best kept to myself, Mister...?"

"Mr Matthew Maidsmead," Maude answered.

Harry laughed in spite of his bad mood.

"That is good! So Mistress Mansfield the maid, becomes Mr Maidsmead the man!"

"I am glad to see a smile on your lips again, Sir Harry."

"Hmm."

They stopped in Witney to take lunch at the Marlborough Inn, but were soon on the road again, leaving the market town behind them. The road followed the path of the Windrush River, the green river valley thick with lush grass and fat sheep. It was a glorious late summer day and even Harry's mood was lifted by the beauty of the surrounding countryside.

The sun was losing its heat as they made their way down the main street of the town of Burford. The warm, yellow stone was lit by the reddening of the sun, so that the town seemed to glow in welcome.

They turned their horses in under an arched gateway and stopped in a small courtyard. A stableboy appeared from a dark corner of the courtyard and took the reins of the horses.

Harry and Maude jumped down on to the smooth flagstones.

"Sir Harry! You are come already! You have made such good time you find me unprepared – you will think me a country bumpkin!"

Maude turned round from her horse to see a handsome lady of middling age approach from the great front door with a wide smile on her lips. Her eyes were bright and her neat dark hair uncovered. She was followed by a scurrying servant.

"My lady de Courcy! How can you say such a thing to me? You know you are my ideal. Why, you make it impossible for any young maid to even hope to catch my eye."

"Harry you are still the rogue as ever, I see," she said with a smile, as Maude frowned sideways at Harry. "It's nice that you do not change."

She looked expectantly at Maude, who faltered slightly under the intense gaze and was instantly anxious about her disguise. John's mother had a keen eye that would obviously miss little.

"May I introduce my clerk, my lady?" Harry said. "This is Mathew Maidsmead. He is hoping to study the law one day himself, but for now he is useful and efficient as a clerk. I let him draw experience as a favour to his father."

"Mr Maidsmead, welcome." The lady eyed Maude curiously. "A handsome youth, Harry. Are you an Oxford man, Mr Maidsmead?"

"Aye, from Oxford ma'am. My father is a glove merchant and an Associate of the Mayor there, so

I hope one day to be able to study the law, as Sir Harry said."

"Mr Maidsmead was very helpful to us in proving your son John's innocence when he was accused of theft last Christmas, Lady de Courcy," Harry added.

"Why then you are doubly welcome, Master Maidsmead. Thank you." She held out her hand to Maude, who took it and bowed slightly in acknowledgment.

"I can see you are the son of a glove maker, Mr Maidsmead. You have the softest hands of any boy I have known."

Maude stared down hard at her hands, to hide her blush.

"There is something... girlish about the boy he has brought as his assistant, Edward," Lady de Courcy said to her husband later. "I never took Harry Hopetoun to have tastes in that direction."

"Nor I," Sir Edward answered. "Indeed, I understood from John that there are feelings between Harry and the younger sister of the Mansfield girl that John's so keen on. I'm sure Harry's as much one for the ladies as ever, my dear."

II

The next morning, Sir Edward accompanied his two young visitors to the Pennyquick house. It was a tall, Cotswold stone building on the main street, rising four storeys from the road. At street level was written 'Pennyquick Parchments' above a smart shop window full of merchandise for anyone who wished to write.

Through the small panes of glass, Maude could see that business was good although it was not yet 9 o'clock in the morning. As Sir Edward entered the shop with his guests, everyone fell silent and bowed to the three 'men'.

"Sir Edward, it is a pleasure. I will call the master's servant," said one of the paper sellers. After a moment, the man returned accompanied by an agreeable-looking man in a leather jerkin. The sort of servant who would engage in any kind of work, inside or out, thought Maude.

"Sir Edward," he said with a slight bow, "The master is expecting you, if you would follow me."

They followed the servant into a corridor and up a narrow, overly-ornate staircase to a miniature hall situated over the paper shop below. The room was flooded with crooked light from the many panes in the windows overlooking the street.

The hall was empty but for a small, round man who had been sitting with his head in his hands. He rose instantly to his feet and arranged the expression on his face, though he was unable to hide the redness of his eyes and nose.

"Sir Edward, welcome."

"Sir Harry Hopetoun, Master Pennyquick, the Oxford scholar with a gift for the law that I was speaking of, and his clerk, Master Maidsmead."

"Gentlemen you are all welcome."

"Master Pennyquick, let me express my deep regret for the grief that has come upon your family," said Harry with a bow.

"And mine, sir," said Maude quietly from under her clerk's cap.

"It is indeed the hardest of blows and I thank you for your interest. Sir Edward tells me you are concerned about the details of my wife's death?"

"I am, sir. It is an unthinkable crime on the roads so close to Oxford and we are keen to find those responsible. If you could repeat all that you know and exactly what you were told by Mr Horniman, the tavern keeper of the Flying Horse, I would be grateful."

"Dear Mr Horniman – he blames himself for what happened because he let her and her nephew travel unaccompanied, but I told him it was not his fault."

"Indeed," said Harry, frowning.

"My dear wife," Mr Pennyquick began, swallowing and swallowing again, pressing his lips together, "was in Oxford, on her way to Highmoor House near Henleigh, the home of her sister. It is a long journey, but she was to spend two nights in Oxford to procure some items, and then proceed to Walling's Ford for a night. From there her sister's man was due to meet her with fresh horses and accompany her and her nephew on to Henleigh. Master Horniman says that they were eager to start travelling early on Tuesday morning and left the tavern before anyone but Horniman was awake. The rest I believe you know and I cannot repeat it."

The man sat back in his chair and sobbed,

"Excuse my conduct, gentlemen, but she was a good, kind woman and the best of wives – and Peter, poor Peter, where is he?"

"There is still no word of him, nor his horse?"

"Nothing. He journeyed via Burford on his way back home especially to accompany his aunt, my dear wife, to Highmoor."

"And your wife, Mr Pennyquick, she was brought home to Burford?"

"She was, on Wednesday, and buried straight away."

"Such haste?"

"It has been unseasonably hot, sir, we could not delay. Mr Horniman recommended that we bury her that very day. His brother-in-law, a holy man, accompanied him especially so that we would not have to wait in case our own minister was away from home. They had secured my good wife in the coffin themselves, to spare us the sight of her poor, beaten body. They were most thoughtful."

"I'll wager they were," said Harry in a way that made Maude look sharply at him.

"But sirs, I forget my manners." Pennyquick pulled the bell rope and the man reappeared. "Gideon, fetch wine and cakes. Master Maidsmead, if you would like to follow Gideon he will give you some refreshment in the kitchen."

Maude's eyes gave nothing away.

"A word, Mathew, if I may before you go," said Harry, raising an eyebrow at Maude. They moved towards the windows while Sir Edward continued to commiserate with Pennyquick.

"Pennyquick was himself a shepherd's son yet sends my clerk to take his wine in the kitchen," whispered Harry. "Are you content to go alone, or shall I make excuses?"

"I am content. I am able to look after myself. This way I may question the servants and check what Pennyquick has said. Engage him in conversation about his wife for a while."

III

"I am sorry for the loss of your mistress, Gideon," said Maude, as she followed him back down the staircase.

"Thank you. It is a sad and sorry business. She was a good mistress, and Master Pennyquick will be lost without her," Gideon replied.

They entered the kitchen at the back of the house, where a cook was at work.

"This is Goodwife Borden, Mr Maidsmead," Gideon introduced her. "Sir Harry Hopetoun's young clerk, Verity. Have we ale and cakes for the boy? Sit yourself down, Mr Maidsmead. You had a long ride of it yesterday, I believe? We saw you come in from the high road in the late afternoon."

Maude sat on a wooden chair and smiled her boyish grin at the pleasant, red-faced Borden as she prepared a tray of wine and cakes for the gentlemen upstairs. Once Gideon had departed with the tray, Borden offered Maude some ale and cake, sitting down opposite her.

"This cake, Goodwife, tastes like nectar!" Maude said, "I have rarely tasted anything better."

"Oh, go on with you, young sir, you jest with me – with all those fancy bakers in Oxford!"

"Fancy they may be. But none can bake like this."

Borden beamed.

"We are all so shocked in the town by this dreadful business, Goodwife Borden. Tell me how it was when poor Mistress Pennyquick's blessed corpse came home."

Gideon re-entered the kitchen as Maude spoke and looked as though he too would answer such an invitation to gossip, but Borden gave him a stern look, then returned to Maude.

"Well, sir! Weren't we in a state? Only four days before, seeing the mistress and young Peter Shackerley leave on their journey to Highmoor House, and now welcoming her back in a box – too, too dreadful! And what of poor Peter? He was the sweetest lad and no one knows where he might be? Who knows what the poor soul may have suffered, or still be suffering!"

Gideon laid a calming hand on Borden's round shoulder.

"There, there Verity, do not upset yourself so. The Lord will be protecting the Mistress's soul and poor Peter Shackerley."

"Then why did He not protect them on the high road, Gideon?"

"Ssh, Verity! Such things are blasphemy, though I know you speak in heat. You must forgive her, sir. She is so put out by this."

"Of course. And still no word about Peter?"

Borden shook her head vigorously, so that her fat cheeks wobbled like her best aspic jelly.

"You'll know, sir, the story of her demise?" offered Gideon. "No one knows if she was attacked by brigands on the road, but the Tavern-keeper said that she was beaten so badly that it would cause too much distress to the master and the children to see her, so they brought her home in a closed box. And only one day dead, yet the smell already so rank it needed more herbs than we could muster, didn't it, Verity?"

Borden nodded enthusiastically.

"He says true, sir. We used all the herbs from the little physic garden the Mistress was so proud of.

Straight in the ground she went, each of us with a herb-filled kerchief to our face, the smell was that bad."

Maude shook her head sympathetically. "A truly terrible business. And can you – either of you – remember anything else about the coffin?"

"Aye, they had travelled a dusty road, sir – it was covered in white dust that won't come off your clothes no matter how much you brush. Look at my coat," Gideon said, taking a coat from a peg on the door and waving it at Maude. "You're a gentleman's man, young sir – can you brush it off?"

Maude looked carefully at the coat and brushed at the dusty marks on it with her hand. She only made it worse. She pursed her lips and frowned, leaning to sniff the persistent white powder on the man's coat, then handed it back with a shrug of defeat and sat down again.

"And why the rushed burial, Goodwife Borden? Mistress Pennyquick must have barely been in the house before she was in the ground?"

"Not in the house *at all,* sir. It was not as we would have liked it to be. There was no wake for her soul. Gideon went to meet the coffin on the road with the master, didn't you, Gideon?"

"I did. Mr Horniman and his brother, the minister, were most insistent that we should not distress ourselves with this dreadful business. His brother was there to perform the ceremony, so no need to call Mr Venal, our own good minister – Mr Venal was most unhappy, I can tell you, when he heard about it. We barely had time to call people from their houses before she was lowered in to the ground."

"But why should your master listen to the Tavern-keeper and his brother?"

"Why they are important men, sir, as might be able to help the master in his business. Mr Horniman is an Associate of the Mayor of the city of Oxford, sir – an Associate of the Mayor, no less – and his brother a holy minister, he said. There is much paper needed in the city of Oxford, sir. A word from these men could make things very easy for the master. And the two of them travelled all that way in a cart to bring the mistress home, sir. Why, we were all quite taken with their kindness, weren't we, Verity?"

The cook pursed her wide lips.

"Not all, Gideon. I did not like the look of the minister especially – he had that look some holy men have, sir, that suggests to a girl that he thinks she has no morals, but at the same time he's eyeing you up as I would a plump chicken for the pot – if you take my meaning, sir."

Maude could not help but snort with laughter.

"My apologies, I should not laugh in a house that is grieving."

"No harm, sir, we know that Verity has her own way with words, don't we, Verity?" said Gideon affectionately smiling at the cook.

IV

The bell sounded and Maude followed Gideon once more up the stairs towards the hall.

"Step in here, for a moment, Master Maidsmead," said Gideon, opening the door to a large dining hall. "The master is most proud of his private sleeping quarter. It is quite the new fashion."

Maude had stopped near the door of the wood-panelled room and was staring up at the painting between the two windows. Her eyes opened wide.

"That is a portrait of the dear Mistress. A striking woman, don't you think? Not that it does her justice..."

"I – I –"

"It is not unusual for men to be lost for words, sir. She was a handsome woman, was she not? And it is a good likeness, God rest her poor soul. It will be a lesser house for her absence."

Maude, still silent, followed Gideon to the hall.

"Ah, Mathew, there you are," Harry said. "We must take our leave. Mr Pennyquick, thank you for your time. Once again, let me express my sorrow."

"You have been most gentle in your questioning, Sir Harry. It has been an honour to talk to you, and of course Sir Edward."

Pennyquick bowed low before the two noblemen.

"*A likeness, Sir Harry*," whispered Maude. "If you remember what the magistrate ordered before we left Oxford?"

Harry looked confused. "Remind me what the *magistrate* said, Mathew."

"The magistrate did most particularly order that we bring a picture of Mistress Pennyquick for the hearing that is to be held in to her sad death."

Harry looked curiously at Maude. "Of course, Mathew. How could I forget such particular instructions. What would I do without you to remind me? Mr Pennyquick, may we borrow a likeness of your dear wife – Sir Edward's son, John, will return it as soon as the magistrate is satisfied?"

"Of course, of course, Sir Harry. I have a likeness here – so like her – you will look after it?"

As Pennyquick handed over the miniature portrait and dissolved in to tears once more, the two of them left him to his grief.

V

"But can you not stay just one more night? It is a long way to ride and you are barely arrived, Sir Harry. Your poor clerk Mr Maidsmead will be tired."

"Why it is Mathew himself who urges me to return today, Lady Mary! If it were up to me I would stay here longer, but Mathew reminds me that there is more to this business than poor Mistress Pennyquick. We are engaged also in a case involving a healing woman who is accused of sorcery."

"A witch? Surely such nonsense is kept for the county of Essex?"

"That's exactly what I said!" Harry laughed. "But it appears that even logic-ruled Oxford is prey to superstition."

"And how does this business with the witch involve you, Sir Harry?"

"She is a trusted servant of my friend, Mistress Maude Mansfield."

Lady Mary raised an eyebrow a fraction. Harry continued quickly.

"The woman also put her life in danger to support John's case against his accusers last Yuletide..."

"*That* lady – the Irishwoman?"

"The same – so Maude and he both believe it is our duty now to help her when she is wrongly accused."

"I would be glad to support her cause, Harry," Lady Mary said. "Tell me – what can I do?"

"You could send a bishop," joked Harry. "They say they will not try her in public without a Bishop to balance out the ways of the devil. Or you could arrange a safe haven for her poor children who are threatened with violence if she pleads innocent."

"*What*? What on earth is going on in Oxford, Harry?"

"A type of madness I think, madam." Maude appeared at the door with the servant behind her. "Mathew, there you are, good. Then we will be on our way to sort the madness as best we can, my lady."

"Wait!" Lady Mary turned and took a small bag from the wooden box on her sewing table. "Defense is not cheap, I know. Take this for her, Harry. Use it in whichever way you think fit. I will send word to our uncle the Bishop in Dorchester to help in the matter if he can."

Lady Mary proferred the bag of coins to Maude.

"You are a trustworthy clerk I think, Mr Maidsmead? Sir Harry seems to depend on you for much."

"I would be happy to be someone such a man as Sir Harry could depend on."

Lady Mary's eyebrows shot up once again.

"*Indeed*? Well, God's speed to you both and God's blessing on your endeavours."

Lady de Courcy stood with her husband watching the pair as they trotted out under the gateway and turned up the road towards Oxford.

"There's something strange about that clerk, my love. I cannot quite put my finger on it..."

VI

"How were my parents?" asked John eagerly, when he met them at the New Inn. The light was gone from the day and night was coming on. Maude was considering how to return home without being seen.

"Very well, John," smiled Harry. "Most hospitable. I was only sad to stay but one night. And so much riding in two days! My arse hasn't felt this bad since I was beaten by Brother Mark for falling asleep in his Latin class."

"Harry! You forget yourself! Or rather you forget there is a lady present..."

"Where? Oh – you mean Mathew? Well, I suppose his arse feels the same. What do you say, Mathew?"

"I say, sir, that this disguise is for the purpose of essential investigation, not to permit rough language, bad manners and references to areas you have no business discussing!"

The two men roared with laughter.

"Oh, stop it – both of you. It has been a long, hard couple of days and I merit kinder treatment," she said. "It is not right to tease a lady so."

"A *lady*? Why Mathew! What *have* you been hiding from me?"

To Harry's surprise, he saw tears beginning to well in the corners of Maude's eyes. The two men attempted to control their smiles.

"John – will you accompany me in through the college gate? I am sorry that your reputation may suffer once again, accompanying a boy in to college this late in the evening, but I can think of no other way to get to Macebius's rooms to change my clothes without being recognised."

"Very well, but you do realise that if this carries on you may have to testify in my defence when I am accused of unnatural acts?"

"Stop!" Maude said, "Enough – before the talk descends into the vile depths once more. Good night, Sir Harry. It has been interesting to be your servant."

"Thank you for your service, Mathew. I look forward to our next meeting."

"In the morning then, Harry, and you must come to me in Macebius's rooms. I cannot come to you."

"*Sir* Harry, Mathew."

"Oh boil your head, you buffoon!" She turned on her heel and marched towards the door with John in pursuit.

Harry watched Maude striding crossly away from him, across the Inn, admiring her elegant legs in her deep crimson doublet and hose, with a concentrated air of contentment on his face.

Chapter 5

I

SUNDAY MORNING dawned a glorious, sunny day. Maude entered the Master's hall for her breakfast walking a little stiffly and frowning.

"Good morrow, Maude," said her father cheerfully. "Your sister said that your aunt's illness was a false alarm, as I might have suspected. She's as strong as an ox that woman. But you need not have hurried back. Why didn't you stay in the country?"

"I wanted to find out how things were with the apothecary woman."

"I have talked to Macebius. He is doing all he can. I do not see that you can do more than he."

"This morning I would go to St Clement's Church across the river."

"Again, Maude?" put in Jane. "Why on earth again?"

"The man Stoneworthy who accuses Susan O'Flaherty is an occasional preacher there. He will no doubt pray there on a Sunday. It might be useful to engage him in conversation, find out more about the case and see what sort of a suspicious fool he is to believe in sorcery."

"I will come with you to the church, Maude," said her father. "I will come and look on the preacher. Then at least I may keep an eye on you, too. Will young Sir Harry be at this particular church, Maude?"

"I think he might, for we are all bent on the same purpose, and John de Courcy too for all I know."

"Do you know – I believe I am strong enough to undertake such a walk myself, this morning," put in Jane. "Sophie can come with us in case I need to return home before you. I will go and tell her to leave her work and prepare herself." Jane bustled quickly out of the room.

"Nothing like the mention of the de Courcy lad to get your sister moving, eh Maude?" laughed Sir Michael as he bit off another mouthful of bread.

II

By the time Jane was content with her appearance they were already late for church. When they had walked at Jane's pace as far as Magdalen Bridge, she had to turn back through fatigue. By the time Maude and her father arrived at St Clement's Church the service was already beginning.

Maude sat, fuming, next to her father. As much as she wished him to do so, Harry Hopetoun, sitting next to John de Courcy five rows in front of them, did not turn towards them. The puritan service was as somber and joyless as any they had ever attended and it was all Maude could do to stay awake through it.

As soon as the Reverend had gone past their pew at the end, Maude pulled on her father's sleeve and they left the church.

"Sir Michael," said the Reverend, bowing over the Master of Christ Church's hand as they exited the church, "a pleasure indeed, sir. To grace our church with..."

"Yes, well – a fine service, Reverend," said Sir Michael and gestured his daughter on to the parched grass of the cemetery, so they could see the congregation as it emerged.

The Reverend Stoneworthy emerged almost immediately after them, and Maude was surprised to see he had a hard-looking, red-faced woman on his arm. Not far behind them came Mr Horniman of the Flying Horse Tavern.

"Why! We have all our players in one place, let the charade begin!" whispered Maude, almost to herself. "Father – that is Stoneworthy with the woman, and behind him Horniman of the Flying..."

Maude stopped as the woman turned at a touch, broke away from Stoneworthy and embraced Horniman. Her hard face improved immeasurably as a smile broke across it. Stoneworthy shook Horniman's hand vigorously, at which point Horniman noticed Maude watching, his eyes lit up and saying something to the group, they moved towards the Mansfields.

"Mistress," said Horniman, "a pleasure to see you again."

"You are, *sir*?" demanded Sir Michael angrily.

"Mr Horniman of the Flying Horse, pleased to make your acquaintance," he turned his charming smile on Maude's father, who was not impressed. "And you are...?"

"Sir Michael Mansfield, Master of Christ Church College, and this, sir, is my daughter. And I would like to know how it is that you seem to *know* my daughter?"

Horniman, Stoneworthy and the woman all gasped slightly at the well-known name.

"Sir Michael! My deepest apologies! I would not have thought to impose upon you – Reverend Stoneworthy and my sister, Agnes Stoneworthy, sir – not at all, but it is a pleasure to speak to you, sir."

"I made enquiries about Susan O'Flaherty, father. I spoke to Mr Horniman in the courtyard of the Inn."

There was a silence as the two parties took in the situation. Stoneworthy could not stand the silence.

"Ah yes, the case of the witch O'Flaherty is a most disturbing one, is it not, Miss Mansfield? You are quite right to be worried about the creature. Sorcery in our own town. I fear it is spreading from the East. You will be pleased to hear that she is awaiting private trial and we hope will be hanged on the morrow."

Maude let out a gasp of horror at this. Agnes Stoneworthy could not help a small but noticeable sneer of contempt curl her lip for one second before she controlled it.

"Tomorrow?" repeated Maude.

"The magistrate has heard that these things tend to breed, one upon another, so he is willing to nip it in the bud. The woman is too full of the devil to allow open court, she may possess others. The case will be heard in private session and the witch will be hanged."

"She shall not, sir!" hissed Maude, as Harry and John joined the party.

"So – you have the Irishwoman hanged already before her trial, Reverend Stoneworthy?" Harry said. "So she can't go curdling your milk again, eh? Of course, milk curdling would have nothing to do with this being the hottest summer in memory, nor your lame horses be due to bad horsemanship?"

"I believe we have met before, young sir – and you are?" said Stoneworthy, drawing himself up to his full height and glaring at Harry.

"Sir Harry Hopetoun, Reverend, and my friend, John de Courcy, Duke's Scholar."

"Sir Harry Hopetoun? John de Courcy?" stuttered Stoneworthy.

Maude saw the sneer transform itself in to a stiff smile as Harry introduced himself. Even Stoneworthy would know Harry's father, Earl Hopetoun. And all the town knew who John was after last Yuletide.

"But why should you gentlemen – why should any of you – be at all interested in an Irish witch?"

"You know what Saint Francis of Assisi says, Reverend." Harry answered, "We just like to help each good soul where we see the need."

"But she is *not* a good soul, sir, she is an *evil* soul that needs to be released from evil."

"We believe not, sir."

"Sir Harry, there is to be a private trial – tomorrow!" said Maude.

"Well we will see you there, Reverend. Until tomorrow then?" Harry gave a slight bow and turned to the Mansfield party who moved majestically away out of the churchyard.

As they went, Maude noticed a member of the church congregation, a rough-looking fellow, who had been watching their conversation. There was something familiar about him. He broke away from the rest of the gathering and followed at a distance.

She told herself to stop imagining things. It could be the man's way home. But why did she feel he was following? She kept close to her father and Sir Harry and walked on at a good pace.

III

"Ha!" Sir Michael shook his head, smiling as they walked. "I wonder which is the greater rogue, Sir Harry, you or that Tavern-keeper? But you took measure of the situation and dealt with it well. I commend you for it."

"And I take a deep pleasure from your words, Sir Michael."

"I'd recommend you desist quoting from the Catholic saints though, Sir Harry, if you want to live a long and happy life with Elizabeth as Queen. Mr de Courcy, how did you enjoy the service?"

"I must admit, sir, I enjoyed the scene we have just witnessed more. Who was the hard-looking woman with them?"

"That, Mr de Courcy, was Agnes Stoneworthy, *sister* of Mr Horniman!" said Maude.

"Agnes Stoneworthy that accuses Susan O'Flaherty is Horniman's *sister*?"

There was a silence as Harry and John took this news in.

"So they are all in league in this business?" John de Courcy said.

"And Pennyquick said that when Horniman came to Burford with the coffin, he came with his brother-in-law, a religious man," Harry added.

"Of course!" said Maude.

"How so – 'of course', Mistress?" glared Sir Michael. "How can you know what this Pennyquick *may* or *may not* have said?"

"Why – because I have told her, sir," put in Harry quickly. "I have tried to keep Mistress Maude informed about all the details of the case."

"But what has this Pennyquick to do with the Irishwoman who you are supporting?" frowned Sir Michael.

"That is what we need to understand, Sir Michael, and by tomorrow morning. We must comprehend what these rogues have been doing. We must have a case to put against Stoneworthy's accusations and his superstitious railing about sorcery."

As the group carried on towards the river and the centre of town, Maude once again noticed the man behind them. She took her father's arm. He looked down at this unusual act of affection and patted her hand.

IV

"Father!" gasped Maude, at the entrance to Christ Church College, realising that the man was now right behind them, "Father – that man!"

The four stopped and turned, Sir Harry and John instantly ready for a fight. The man looked terrified and put up his hands in surrender.

"Here – I know you, don't I?" Harry said, looking closer at him.

"I thought the same, Sir Harry – he has been following us," Maude added.

"Barkis, sir, mistress," the man said, removing his cap. "Bargee, sir, what delivers coal on the river, sir."

He looked toward John de Courcy and explained,

"When your good self was in a bit of trouble last year, sir, it was I what delivered Mistress O'Flaherty to the courtroom, hidden in one of my sacks of coal, sir*"

Harry slapped his thigh.

"Ha! Of course! I knew I had seen you before – but last time you were so covered in coal-dust that one could have taken you for a Moor! This man helped save your neck, Johnny!"

* See *The Fortunes of John de Courcy* in the Paper Planes collection.

"Mr Barkis, I am eternally thankful to you," said John kindly. "What is it you want from us?"

"Begging your pardons, sirs, mistress, but I have come in the case of my good friend Mrs O'Flaherty. I think you know already – she has been taken by the bailiffs, sir, and is to be tried as a witch."

"We know of this, Barkis. We have been doing all we can to help her. Why do you come to us now?"

"I heard through an acquaintance of Master Macebius, sir, him as is a good friend to Susan, that you might be taking an interest in her case. I believe I have information, sir, that might help her, but am not certain of it."

"Information? What sort of information, Barkis?"

"From the river folk, sir. We are a close community and I have been making enquiries of my own, though I be no legal man. Would you listen to me, sirs, mistress?"

"We will Barkis, and without delay. Follow us – we will go to Macebius, so that he too may listen in on this man's news."

Chapter 6

I

ALDERMAN BAILEY WAS ARRANGING his magistrate's robes in one of the small ante-rooms to the court, and would not appear in the courtroom for a while. As this was to be a closed trial, bailiffs stood at the door and prevented anyone from entering.

It seemed that word about Susan O'Flaherty's trial had spread. Half the town was there. The boat people who lived and worked on the river had come in their Sunday best.

At the request of the coal-man Barkis they had worked hard in the last twenty four hours to persuade anyone who had ever been treated by Susan O'Flaherty to be there. Grateful prostitutes who had not bothered to go to bed stood brightly dressed and yawning amongst the crowd of poorly-dressed townsmen and women, like kingfishers in a flock of starlings.

There was a respectful distance kept from Maude and her band of defenders on one side of the hallway and from Stoneworthy, Horniman and their supporters on the other. All looked nervous. All but Macebius who, as always, was perfectly calm.

"Are you sure of your uncle, John?" Macebius asked.

"I am, sir. He is a busy man, of course, but my mother sent me word – he will be here."

There was a commotion in the sunshine outside the high doorway. A noise of a cart stopping and battling cries of "Witch!", "Cruel gaolers! What have you done to her?" and "Poor innocent!" fought for supremacy as bailiffs, the gaoler from Bocardo and Susan O'Flaherty herself appeared in the doorway.

The spectators gasped at the sorrowful sight. Susan was filthy, her hair matted and ragged. The smell coming from her made the crowd draw back and leave a good space around her. She stood hunched over due to the pain of her ribs where she had been beaten. The bruises on her face had faded to a pale green and purple, giving her the appearance of someone already dead.

"Make way! Make way for the prisoner!" shouted the bailiff self-importantly.

While all stepped back, Maude stepped forward.

"Susan," she whispered. "Your children are safe. You must believe me. Your children are safe. You can speak in your defence. You *must* speak..."

"No talking with the prisoner! Get back, Mistress! I will not ask you twice!"

"Shut your mouth, you festering codpiece!" shouted Harry, much to the crowd's delight. "Don't you dare talk to a lady in that manner or I'll make you wish your mother had never coupled with the goblin that must have been your father."

"I'll have you arrested, Sir Harry, for all your fine garments," shouted Horniman at Harry.

"*You,* sir? I think not. If any man is to be arrested today it will be you, Mr Horniman!"

A shadow flickered briefly across Horniman's face as the crowd roared its approval at the entertainment. In the second's distraction lent by the warring males, Maude caught and held the eye of Susan O'Flaherty.

"Believe me," she mouthed at Susan's desperate expression.

Alderman Bailey appeared at the officials' entrance in his magistrate's finery, frowning in bewilderment at the noise and shouted for quiet.

"Due to the evil and devilish nature of the accused..."

"Rubbish!" shouted someone in the crowd, others joining in and other cries of "Shame on you!" and "Codswallop!" ran through the throng.

"...due to the evil and devilish nature of the accused... this will be a private hearing in front of the Magistrate only, his officers and those who accuse the witch, so that the devil cannot work his evil magic amongst the townspeople..."

"Too late!" shouted someone and the crowd dissolved in to laughter.

"Silence!" shouted Alderman Bailey, banging his staff of office on the stone flags. "The verdict shall be announced to the people once the fate of the prisoner is decided."

"It sounds as if she is condemned by you before she is heard, Bailey," said a sonorous voice at the back of the crowd.

The heads all turned towards the voice and gasped as they saw the figure of a Bishop standing there dressed in his robes of office.

Bailey looked confused.

"Your Grace?"

The Bishop of Dorchester, John de Courcy's uncle, laughed.

"Surprised to see me, eh, Bailey? I heard you had a problem with Beelzebub and as I was in the town, thought I would come to help. Now that I am here to defend you all from the *alleged* devil possessing this poor woman, I presume it is safe to let us all in to the courtroom to hear your fair trial, sir?"

The Bishop fixed Bailey with his eye, and Bailey visibly gulped before glancing angrily towards Horniman, who was looking similarly surprised.

"My Lord Bishop," began Horniman, bowing to the Bishop, "this is an unimportant case, an unimportant witch, not something to trouble a great man like yourself, my Lord, who must have many other matters to look to more important than this one?"

"And men more important than you, whomever you may be..."

"Horniman, your Grace, *Associate* of the *Mayor*"

"Indeed. Fascinating. So let us start this superstitious charade. Lead the way, Bailey."

Horniman, his face like thunder, strode towards Susan as she was led in to the courtroom.

"They will burn, witch, all three of them, remember that," he hissed. "One word and your children will burn."

Susan's eyes opened in terror. She looked for Maude, who had seen Horniman's whispered words, and whose face was set in an anxious frown.

II

"Clerk, the case against the accused, if you please?" Bailey shouted over the noise of the crowd, banging his hammer for silence.

The noise died down as the Clerk got to his feet.

"Susan O'Flaherty of 15 Paradise Alley is accused of Maleficium under the 1562 Witchcraft Act, as passed by Her Majesty's Parliament."

"Plain English if you please, Mr Clerk, so the people can understand?" said Bailey, who could not understand a word of Latin, being a simple butcher who, like his animals, had grown fat on the pastures seized from monasteries in the 1540s.

"Maleficium, sir," said the Clerk wearily (he was an educated man and unimpressed by Alderman Bailey's airs of grandeur), "is the use of diabolical powers to do harm to others or their property."

"And who is the accuser of the witch?"

Macebius stood up. "It is not legal to refer to her as a witch until the accusation has been proven in a court of law. You are in contempt, Mr Bailey, by speaking so."

Bailey's eyes narrowed at the figure of Macebius.

"I? The Magistrate? In contempt? And you are?"

"Macebius of Christ Church College, late of Lincoln's Inn, Professor at philosophy and law. I am defending the plaintiff."

"*Defending*? There has been no talk of *defending*! By what right and at whose bidding are you doing this defending, Master Macebius?" spluttered Bailey.

"May I remind you, Mr Bailey, that the law is in place for defending the rights of the weak, not to protect those in positions of power..."

The crowd cheered loudly in agreement.

"...and it seems to me that in this situation the weak have no defence against those in power in this town. Therefore I, and my colleagues are here to mount a defence."

"Your *colleagues*? What, there's more of you?" said Horniman looking round.

"I am aided by the able investigations of..."

Bailey banged his hammer again.

"Enough! We'll miss luncheon if this carries on. You told me this was a simple case, Horniman. It seems not." Bailey sighed heavily. "Let's get on with it. On what evidence is she accused?"

"On mine, sir," said Stoneworthy getting to his feet, sticking out his chest like a cockerel and taking the oath.

"And your accusations are what, Reverend Stoneworthy?"

"This woman, in league with the powers of darkness, to gain revenge against my poor wife, sir, made my horses lame. Also, sir, she has curdled the milk in my dairy, she has conjured my butter churn and she has put a sickness upon my wife, sir!"

"And the reason for this?"

"Why, my poor wife did consult her for a case of the wind, sir."

The crowd laughed and Agnes Stoneworthy glared at her husband.

"And the witch gave her herbs to help her flatulence which did not help, so Agnes, my good wife, sir..."

"Yes, Stoneworthy – I've known Agnes for years, there's no need for silly detail," grumbled Bailey.

"Well, Agnes did return to the witch and tell her the herbs were no good – the problem was still with her - and so the witch put spells upon us and our goods, sir and must be hanged for Maleficium, like the Clerk said."

"I said nothing of the sort, Reverend Stoneworthy," said the Clerk sharply, "I simply announced the accusations against the poor woman. I didn't agree with them."

"And does your wife support these accusations, Reverend?" asked Bailey.

"I do, sir!" said Agnes, getting to her feet.

There was a cry of "How's the wind, Agnes?" and "Open a window someone!" from the crowd, which set the people laughing once again and Agnes blushing as red as a ripe apple.

Bailey banged his hammer, shouting, "One more interruption and you're all out – not including *your Grace* of course –" he added to the Bishop, who was sitting on a great, wooden chair, looking unamused.

"And there are others too sir," Agnes continued, "who have had the same misfortune at the hands of the Irishwoman."

There were cries of "Aye!" and "Witch!" from characters around Agnes.

"She is a witch, sir, plain as day, and in our town too."

"Enough, Agnes!" said Stoneworthy sternly, and she sat down again, looking crushed.

"Let's get her up here and see if we can get this hanging done before luncheon," said Bailey, gesturing at Susan O'Flaherty.

The crowd fell to silence as the guards pulled Susan to her feet and she made her way slowly to the side of Bailey's heavy table.

"What have you to say to these accusations, woman?" said Bailey roughly.

Susan was silent.

"Susan – speak!" commanded Maude.

All eyes turned in the silence to see who had spoken and then returned to the sorry sight of the silent plaintiff.

"Will you say nothing in your defence, Mrs O'Flaherty?" asked Bailey impatiently. "Well, then all I can do..."

"I would say something in her defence, Magistrate Bailey," said Macebius getting to his feet.

Bailey sighed and rested his chin on his hand, staring at Macebius.

"And will it be much, sir?" he asked with a sigh.

"It may well be, Magistrate."

III

Macebius looked around the room before he began. All eyes and ears were his.

"Susan O'Flaherty has lived in this town for a number of years. In that time she has been an obedient citizen. She has shown no sign of the baser instincts required to prove a case of Maleficium, no damage to people or property in that time."

Bailey looked confused already.

"She is a talented healer. There are many as would vouch for that, myself amongst them. She has helped many, including the wife of her own gaoler, I believe?" Macebius glanced across at the man, who nodded enthusiastically, glad to have been brought to notice, until he caught sight of the thunder on Horniman's face, and stopped nodding.

"She has been an obedient, quiet widow and a good mother to her three young children. She has attended church every week."

"Yes, yes, so what of all this? If she won't open her mouth to defend herself, then she condemns herself by her silence. That is the law. Even you, *Professor*, cannot change the law." said Bailey impatiently.

"I mean not only to highlight the improbability of the accusations, Mr Bailey, but also to prompt Mrs O'Flaherty to open her mouth and proclaim herself 'not guilty', with the help of Mistress Mansfield, here."

"Mistress Mansfield? What have you to do with this?"

"I am the last person to see Mrs O'Flaherty before she went to the Flying Horse Tavern and was then arrested," said Maude.

"Lies!" shouted Horniman, getting to his feet. "Why do you people persist in this falsehood? I have told you there was no visit to the Flying Horse. There are no witnesses."

"Witnesses may be paid – or threatened – to hold their tongue Mr Horniman," said Maude looking him straight in the eye. She laid her hand on the bible that the Clerk held up and took the oath.

Bailey shook his head and frowned.

"What has any of this to do with whether this woman is or is not a witch?"

"We mean to prove that she was arrested and accused following her visit to the Flying Horse, to stop her talking about what she had seen there."

"And what had she seen there, pray, Mr Macebius?" asked Bailey.

"We do not know, Mr Bailey, beyond treating a sick woman."

"There *was* no sick woman!" shouted Horniman again. "I would know if there was sickness in my own tavern!"

"Horniman, patience please. We have to act as a court of law," pleaded Bailey.

"Aye – if you can act, sir," put in Harry. "You seem like a poor band of players to me." The crowd laughed appreciatively.

"Silence. Enough of your insolence, young man. Clerk – make a note of his name! What's your name?"

"Sir Harry Hopetoun, your servant, sir," said Harry facetiously, bowing low.

Bailey mopped his furrowed brow with his handkerchief.

"Sir Harry Hopetoun too?" Bailey muttered desperately. "Aye well – I'll have order in my court. Whoever next?"

"Get on with it, Bailey!" shouted the Bishop. "If you cannot control your own court I will have to take your place. I do not have all day to defend you all from this alleged devil."

IV

Maude walked over to Susan and laid a hand on her arm.

"Susan," she said. "Look at me."

Susan raised her head and Maude felt her heart contract at the pitiful sorrow she saw in the other woman's eyes.

"You must trust me, Susan. It is safe for you to speak. You must trust me."

"They are all alone, Mistress, my sweet infants. You are here. Who's there to defend them?"

"Just trust me, Susan. Will you answer with your plea?"

Silence.

"Will you, Susan?"

"Not guilty," whispered Susan finally, her eyes racked with fear and a desperate anxiety.

Across the room Horniman nodded inconspicuously to a man by the door, who turned and nodded to someone out of sight in the street. The Bishop noted all this without a flicker crossing his expression.

"There. That wasn't too hard, was it? Now you know Mr Macebius to be a good man, don't you?" said Maude softly.

Susan nodded, tears of anxiety streaming down her dirty face.

"You can tell him all that happened on last Monday night."

"A man came to the house, sir, before the great storm. I had to come, he said, as fast as ever I could move, to the Flying Horse, and I was to tell no one. He said there was a sick lady.."

"Bailey, I..." Horniman began, but was interrupted by the Bishop.

"Oh do shut up and sit down before I have you taken to the Tower, you rogue!" the Bishop shouted.

"Carry on, Mrs O'Flaherty."

Susan gulped. "I packed my healing bag and ran out in to the storm. On Brewer Street I bumped in to Mistress Mansfield there, and forgetting what the man had said, told her where I was going, but swore her to secrecy."

"Do you confirm this, Mistress Mansfield? You are under oath." asked Bailey.

"I do, Mr Bailey."

"And so, Mrs O'Flaherty?" ventured Macebius kindly.

"When I got to the Tavern, I was met by the same messenger, I do not know his name, and shown to a chamber upstairs where I found a lady, dreadful sick, sir. I told the man it was the pestilence, sir..."

The crowd erupted with cries and roars of horror. The plague? In the city?

"Liar! The woman's a liar! Pestilence? In my tavern?" roared Horniman.

"Fire!" came a cry from outside. "Fire! Fire in Paradise!"

Susan's face turned white as she turned towards the cry. Chaos broke out as the crowd bundled out of the courtroom to help. Fire was everyone's greatest fear. The city was so dry that fire would spread quickly if it were not brought under control.

"Watch the prisoner!" shouted Bailey jumping to his feet also, removing his coat and rushing out with the rest. He had property in Paradise Street.

Susan had sunk back against the Clerk's table.

"No!" she whispered.

"No," echoed Maude, who had not moved a muscle. "Trust me, Susan. They are safe."

"But won't they be trapped?"

Maude pursed her lips and shook her head.

"They are not there. Nor are many of your herbs and potions."

The Bishop got to his feet and rubbed his hands.

"This really is the most extraordinary spectacle. Even if we don't root out the rot in this town, which I think we are about to do, this is worth the ride from Dorchester. But a welcome adjournment.

A mug of wine and a biscuit or two, I think, before we reconvene, eh, Mistress Mansfield?"

Maude smiled. "It will be a pleasure for me to bring you some from the College, Bishop, for all the others will be fighting the fire."

Chapter 7

I

"ONLY THE THREE HOUSES DAMAGED. The humid terrain down in Paradise meant the fire could not take hold before the good people of the town brought it under control with water from the Castle stream. But the house where it started badly damaged, sir."

"Do we know whose house it is? Was there anyone inside?"

"It was the house of the witch, sir – Mrs O'Flaherty. Someone suggested that the devil himself set it alight with the fire of hell!"

The Bishop raised an eyebrow and looked extremely sceptical.

"I think it is far more likely to have been the two fellows seen running from the scene by at least five witnesses, or so I have been told. They have been taken and are being guarded closely, is that right, Clerk?"

"It is, your Grace. We will deal with them later, apply certain methods which may encourage them to say who put them up to this deed. They could have destroyed the whole town if the fire had caught!"

Horniman's face was a strange shade of pale. He sat silently, impassive, as Macebius got to his feet and approached Susan again.

"So, Mrs O'Flaherty, you had just identified the pestilence in the lady – this lady that Mr Horniman says is an invention of yours? He claims there was no sick lady at the Flying Horse, what say you to that, Mrs O'Flaherty?"

"I know what I saw, sir. There was a lady sick at the Flying Horse that night and I have seen the pestilence before. There are different types of the plague, sir, and this was a most vicious kind, although not strongly contagious. There is no mistaking it."

"And this lady who allegedly did not exist, Mrs O'Flaherty. Can you describe her?"

"Fair enough lady, around thirty five or so in age, I'd say, well-built, but I would know her again in an instant, sir..."

"Really? How so?"

"She had the mark of the Virgin in her hair, sir!"

"Explain what you mean, for those who do not know the Virgin's mark."

"Well she had dark hair, sir, a beautiful head of dark hair, and at the front a strong streak of white, sir. 'Tis said it is where the Virgin has touched you – very lucky it's meant to be, although not for this poor lady, it seems."

Macebius took a miniature portrait from Maude and showed it to Susan.

"Do you recognise the woman in this picture, Mrs O'Flaherty?"

"Why, that is her! That's the woman! The very woman! How did you get this, sir? Where? Who?"

"What is this sorcery?" thundered Horniman. "There was no picture!"

All eyes turned to where Horniman stood, red-faced, breathing deeply. Stoneworthy looked straight ahead, eyes fixed, mouth as taut as a cow's arse.

"There was no picture – *where* – Mr Horniman?" asked Macebius very slowly.

"Why, I did not mean that. I meant that there was no *woman*, so how could there be a picture of her?"

No one was convinced.

"Oh, I believe there was indeed a woman, Mr Horniman. Take the oath, sir, if you will. Though I doubt an oath of yours will make much difference to the tale you tell," added Macebius under his breath as Horniman took the oath.

"There was a woman called Mistress Pennyquick staying in your tavern that night, you will agree with that, I believe, for we all know the sad tale of Mrs Pennyquick, who galloped off from your tavern early on Tuesday morning, accompanied by her young nephew. She was cruelly attacked and murdered, and her nephew is nowhere to be found, is that not so?"

“Aye, sir, but what’s the unfortunate Mistress Pennyquick got to do with the witch’s lies? She has invented this story of the plague to do me harm, sir, just like she did harm to my poor sister and the good Reverend Stoneworthy. As Agnes is my sister, the witch is trying to do me in as well by saying there was pestilence in my tavern. ‘Tis a rotten and evil thing to do and she must be hanged for it!”

Macebius was leaning against the back of a heavy, wooden chair, staring at Horniman as he said his piece, eyebrows raised.

“Finished, Horniman? Good. The picture Mrs O’Flaherty identified as the lady she treated for plague in the Flying Horse, was Mistress Pennyquick, given to my colleagues by Mistress Pennyquick’s own husband.”

The mood in the room changed suddenly as the crowd erupted into shouts and cries. Plague in the town was what everyone feared. First fire and now plague. This was not the entertainment they had expected.

“Quiet!” shouted Mr Bailey, his brow now furrowed with anxiety rather than anger. This was not how they had planned the trial should go. "Order!" he roared, banging his hammer.

"I am confused, Master Macebius. Explain, if you will."

"It was Mrs Pennyquick that Susan O'Flaherty was called to treat at the Flying Horse a week ago. She did indeed have some form of the pestilence about her, which caused her and her nephew to die that night. Her nephew had lately come from Bristol, where it is said a plague landed with a ship from Venice. So it is likely the nephew that infected her."

"Susan O'Flaherty was dismissed as soon as she declared the pestilence. Horniman, realising that this could bring ruin to his business, and ruin to many of his friends, had Susan seized by the bailiffs on the way home and taken to Bocardo. There, she was threatened with the death of her children – by burning – if she spoke a word of what she had seen that night."

"So Mr Horniman is left with a body – worse – two pestilential bodies and the threat of ruin. What can he do?"

"Bailey, stop this evil invention," shouted Horniman pointing at Macebius. "This man is in league with the devil too! He is part of the plot, the sorcery! Arrest this devil!"

"Horniman, you are embarrassing yourself," said the Bishop quietly, "If you want to avoid being dragged out in to the public street to be whipped, hung, drawn and quartered, right now, I suggest you sit down and keep silence."

II

"The roads out of town are all patrolled at night, but by men in the pay of Horniman," Macebius continued. "They would not question their paymaster, taking a barrel of ale from the town in the night. Mr Barkis, bring your witness forward if you will?"

Barkis the bargee stepped forward from the crowd, leading another boatman by the arm.

"Your name, man?"

"Beesley, sir." The man had removed his cap to expose filthy hair that someone had attempted to neaten and flatten.

"Take the oath, Beesley."

"Now tell us what you saw last Monday night, Beesley. Remember you have taken an oath on the holy bible, so only the absolute truth." Macebius smiled kindly at the terrified Beesley.

"I was on my skiff, sir, drifting in the Christ Church stream, sir, as I like to do some nights when I can't sleep. The storm had passed and the air fresher than it had been for weeks, sir. A lovely night it was, although still dark with cloud."

"What time of the night was this, Beesley?"

"Well past midnight and heading towards dawn, sir. I heard a sound on the water, some kind of boat heading up from the Magdalen Bridge. I was worried it might be thieves or villains, sir, I let myself drift towards the mouth of the stream where it meets the river, and pulled myself in amongst the reeds there."

"And that's when I spied Mr Horniman, sir, and another man, coming down the river with a large beer barrel on their boat. I thought that was strange, moving barrels of ale at this time of night when there is little light to guide you – why would they do such a thing? Why not wait till dawn? The river is a dangerous place, sir, if you do not know her humours."

"And you know how sometimes you can just feel that something is not quite right? Well, there was something about Mr Horniman and his companion that didn't feel right, so I thought I would follow them, sir, just to see what was what. I floated down-river after them, keeping them in sight, but I believe they did not see me, sir."

"We went some way downstream, passed Iffley and on. Then they carried on to the place they call Sandy Ford, just south of the town, sir."

"There was some light in the sky now, so once again I hid among the reeds and watched as they struggled with one of the large barrels, sir, rolling it up the bank and away out of sight. But the strange thing was that they had cloths tied over their hands like mittens, and when they came back without the barrel, I saw a spark and then a small fire – just there by the bank – and they pulled the cloths off their hands and dropped them in the fire to burn."

III

As Beesley finished his story there was complete silence throughout the courtroom. Outside the open windows the cries and noises of the town could be heard, but inside the room the people seemed to have stopped breathing.

Beesley replaced the cap on his head and returned to his place in the still crowd.

Mr Bailey was looking confused.

"But I don't understand, the horse came back without her."

"Only by Horniman's word, Mr Bailey," said Macebius. "No one saw the lady and her nephew leave the Tavern. I'm sure at least one, simple-headed groom in Horniman's employ will swear he saw her horse return to its stable, but there is no note of a riderless horse passing through the East-gate in to town on the morning of Tuesday last."

Horniman sat with his face in his hands.

"I would suggest to this gathering, that the barrel seen by Beesley contained the remains of Mistress Pennyquick. We have yet to discover what happened to poor Peter Shackerley's body, his personal effects and his fine horse. Mrs Pennyquick's body was taken to a spot near Sandy Ford, where she could conveniently be 'found' by Mr Horniman the next day, without the observers or difficult questions he would face in the town."

"The same Mr Horniman, then sealed her so tightly in her limed coffin that no curious person would be able to remove the lid without destroying the box. He took it from there to Witney, taking a Cleric along with him, where he stayed overnight, and then on to Burford the next day. In Burford, he so effectively charmed Mr Pennyquick, using Pennyquick's respect of Horniman's position in Oxford as a bribe to buy poor Pennyquick's silent acceptance of the story. Pennyquick was foolishly struck by the kindness of the Inn-keeper and his Reverend brother Stoneworthy, bringing Mrs Pennyquick's body home themselves all the way to Burford. Pennyquick, overcome by grief, followed their advice about the effect of the hot weather on the body and she was put in the ground before the day was out."

"Buried before the day was out, without even entering the walls of her own home and with barely time to summon some members of her family and friends to her graveside. But not before the servants had noticed the stench coming from her coffin and the white powder of lime that got in to their eyes and nose and clothes, as lime will. Still on the coat of Pennyquick's man-servant days later, I believe, Mistress Mansfield?"

Maude nodded in agreement.

"Like the plague, it is persistent stuff and clings like the stench of guilt on a man, eh Horniman? Stoneworthy?"

"So what is the real issue we are staring at here? Murder?" asked the Bishop.

"No sir! Not murder!" cried Horniman jumping to his feet. "The pestilential boy and foolish woman died in my tavern. Is it a crime to merely transport bodies somewhere else?"

Macebius's eyes opened wide at the naivety of the Inn-keeper.

"Aye sir, it is. Moving plague victims through the town without due precaution, not declaring the plague in the town, therefore putting the whole town at risk, disposing of the boy Heaven knows how, obstructing the truth about the woman's death, inventing a crime involving an attack on said woman and a robbery which never actually existed – interfering with the proper burial of a plague victim, wrongfully accusing an innocent woman of sorcery and happy to see her hanged for it, setting fire to her house with intent to..."

"That was not me! I was here – everyone saw I was here..."

"Oh yes, we saw *you* were here, Horniman, but I think we will find the two villains who set the fire are already prepared to trade the identity of their employer for a lesser sentence. As I was saying – setting fire to Mrs O'Flaherty's house with the intent of murdering her children, who you had checked were inside..."

The crowd gasped in horror at this and whispered amongst themselves – burning children alive? They stared at Horniman as if afraid of what he might do next.

"I can confirm the children were not in fact inside. But you were not to know that, eh Horniman? I can see by your expression that it comes as a surprise to you now. What sort of a man are you,

Horniman? And you, Stoneworthy? A supposed man of God, supporting such evil crimes."

"Enough!" shouted the Bishop, getting to his feet. "The rotten authority in this town makes me sick! Bailey, dismiss the case against the woman. Guards – arrest these two men, and the wife happy to perjure for her brother. If evil runs in families, let their family end here, for the town cannot support more of their kind. Take them away."

There was an eruption of noise and activity as the crowd rushed out to spread the word throughout the town – plague! The Mayor himself in league with criminals!

Epilogue

As Susan O'Flaherty had no home to return to, Maude took her to the servants' quarters in the college, and gave her to one of the servant girls to help wash off the stench of the prison and put her into an old gown of Maude's.

Maude returned to find a very different looking Susan waiting for her.

"Why, Susan, you look quite the lady! Come, let's see how those children are faring."

Maude led the way across to Macebius's rooms, where they found the three children sitting in a row on the window seat, obviously terrified by the men around them. Macebius was smiling down at them. Harry and John were drinking wine from metal goblets.

"Do you know," Macebius said, as the children rushed over to their mother and flung their arms round her, "they hadn't moved a muscle. Just like I told them. Just sat there, while we argued that chaos out in the courtroom."

"Didn't I tell you what a good mother Susan is?" smiled Maude, staring at the little group of mother and children, crying and kissing and hugging each other for joy.

"So how did you rescue them, Maude?" asked Harry. "I presume it was you? All this time the town is looking at Mrs O'Flaherty as a sorceress and yet you seem to have powers to spirit children out of houses under the very noses of the villains watching the place. I wouldn't even have known where the children were. Did you smuggle them out when it was dark?"

"I couldn't bring them out – there were men watching the house at all times. They thought they were well-hidden, but Horniman does not hire the cleverest of men. They watched me going in to the house with my baskets of food and they watched me come out, not knowing I was taking baskets of precious herbs and potions with me."

"I trusted that as long as they saw me emerge – leaving the three children – they would not be suspicious."

"You know the stories about tunnels – from the times when the Jews lived and worked in the town? Macebius here taught me the labyrinth of tunnels, one house to another, when I was a child. A tunnel runs also from the old Greyfriars monastery to what was St Frideswide's Priory – here, beneath our very feet."

"The houses in Paradise Street are all linked through their attics, so I led the children through the attics to the last house – whether anyone was in the house we do not know, we were quiet as mice, weren't we? Through to the back yard, and then to the Greyfriars' tunnel. The brave children went through the tunnel on their own with a lit torch, met by Macebius at this end, while I returned the way I had come, emerged from the house with my basket and the watchmen didn't know a thing."

"Such courage is unusual in such small children," said John admiringly.

"Clarity did cry a little in the tunnel sir, but we encouraged her and she did stop," said Patrick seriously.

"You are a kind and clever boy, Patrick." Macebius patted the boy on the head.

"We must find somewhere for you all to live, Mrs O'Flaherty, until we can force Horniman to pay for the damage he has caused," said John.

Susan blushed.

"Well, sir, you are kind to think of us, but Mr Barkis, the boatman, he has long been persuading me he is the man to marry. I was happy in my home on dry land, but he is a good man, and the children are fond of him, and I can see he has worked hard to clear my name. So now that we are homeless, it seems like a good time to finally give in to the man. So we will be living on the river, sir."

The three children gasped with excitement and clasped their mother's hands tighter.

After Susan and the children had shut the door behind them, Macebius, Maude, Harry and John sat at Macebius's table and re-filled their goblets with his fine wine.

"To Justice!" said Maude, lifting her goblet.

"To Justice indeed," John added. "We have saved the life of a good woman and her children. You put yourself at risk to get them to safety and find the truth in this business, Mistress Maude."

"Ah yes – the risk of marriage to Sir Harry here, if my disguise had been discovered."

"That was indeed a danger you faced courageously!" laughed John.

"But I made a credible clerk, it seems."

"Except it's a pity that you were so duped by the charms of Horniman of the Flying Horse," put in Harry. "To listen to you, the man was a saint."

"I named him no saint, Sir Harry," said Maude indignantly. "Simply charming, that's all. And quite handsome..."

"*Handsome*? That dog? Mistress Maude I fear you need eye-glasses!"

"'Tis good the villain's charms did not impede your vision of right and wrong, Mistress Maude," put in John. "Harry, I fear you are biased in your appraisal. Are you envious of Horniman's apparent charms?"

Harry picked up a piece of bread and threw it – hard – at John.

Maude looked around her and clapped her hands excitedly.

"My father must have forgotten about me in all the excitement – it is unlike him to let me be without a chaperone these days."

"What need for a chaperone with honourable gentlemen like us?" said Harry.

"You?" said John. "Rumour has it you have been consorting with boys out in country towns. Very pretty boys too, it appears. I do believe my mother was a little suspicious of your tastes, from the tone of her letter to me about your pretty clerk."

Harry looked shocked as the others roared with laughter.

"Surely she cannot suspect that I...?"

Maude's face was suddenly alive with laughter. "There was I so worried that I might be found out and forced to marry you, Harry, and instead you are suspected of some monkish games with your clerk! Ha!"

"Maybe Lady Mary is more perceptive than you hoped, Sir Harry," began Macebius, "about your intentions towards your clerk..."

Maude looked in to her goblet, blushing, and then got swiftly to her feet.

"Before I get in any more trouble and am locked up in a nunnery for my pains, I had better return to the Master's lodgings. Good day gentlemen," said Maude, trying to hide her blushes and rushing from the room.

"Was that a blush I spied in the soft cheek of Mistress Maude as she fled?" cooed John. "And also on the cheek of our friend Harry, Macebius?"

"I believe it was, Mr de Courcy," Macebius answered, "I believe the pretty young sorceress herself may be falling under the spell of a certain young scholar, who is himself under her spell..."

Harry pushed his chair back and stood up angrily.

"If you two have had enough of your jesting at my expense, I have philosophical arguments that I must master for my tutorial, do I not, Master Macebius? I will apply myself to them. You will be lenient with the timing of my essay, sir?" asked Harry haughtily.

"Not at all. No concessions for gallivanting around the country with attractive legal clerks, Sir Harry. I expect the work here, tomorrow noon at the latest!" Macebius banged his hand on his desk to make his point.

Harry threw on his cloak and stormed from the room.

John and Macebius sat, laughing gently, as the door slammed.

"Shall we lay a wager, John? How long it will take the sorcery to work its spell, for them to declare their feelings for each other? What say you to a sovereign they are betrothed before a year is out?"

John held out his hand. "I'll say it'll take longer!"

"Done!"

If you enjoyed this book, don't miss the other titles from the **paper planes** collection.

Here is an excerpt from:

Two Kinds of Dying

Graham Hurley

Introduction

THIS IS AN IMAGINING. It was inspired by the events that surrounded my father's death, and it's based on months of reading, archival research, and face-to-face conversations. As Dad's only daughter, for reasons that I still can't explain to myself, it felt right for me to try and join the many pieces that comprise the strangeness of his life. The dates and the locations are real, as were the tides of history that swept him into captivity. The rest, I confess at once, is my version of what may have happened. The more I followed my father's wartime journey, the better I felt I understood the man he became. That I may also have accidentally discovered a larger truth – that we are all the prisoners of our past – is for you to judge.

Chapter 1 Dad and Teazle

I FIRST PICTURE MY FATHER in the winter of 1939-40. I have a photograph, which helps enormously. He's 19, skinny, on the short side, and absurdly handsome. The war is a couple of weeks old and he's just answered the nation's call to arms. The fact that he wears his beret at a defiantly jaunty angle, and that the top buttons of his khaki blouse are undone, suggests that he has yet to confront the darker realities of army life. In the background is the seafront at Clacton-on-Sea, which I remember from my own youth. My first real taste of fear was the afternoon Dad took me on the Big Wheel at the amusements. He loved fairgrounds and probably, at this point in his young life, regarded the war as one long free ride.

In the photo, Teazle stands beside him. He looks twice the size of Dad. Twenty mile route marches have yet to make any impact on his girth and he has the same blind faith that everything, the war included, will turn out just fine. One arm lies lightly across Dad's slender shoulders. Like Dad, he's playing up for the camera. These two men, in their sepia innocence, love each other.

The regimental depot for the 7th Royal Sussex Regiment is in Brighton, where both Dad and Teazle live. Neither of them have any money, an oversight that the war will do absolutely nothing to correct, but Dad has borrowed a handful of money from a mate, and he and Teazle have set out to drink it all. In later life, Dad loved a glass or two of beer, a habit that I like to think started early. It's spring at last, after a savage winter. A strong rumour suggests the regiment are about to entrain for Southampton Docks, and thence to France. As it turns out, the rumour is true. This is the last time Dad will see the inside of an English pub for quite a while.

Dad adored pickled onions. He ate them all his life. There's a big jar of them on the pub counter, and another one, full of pickled eggs, beside it. Teazle orders two of both.

"You're crazy, you are. That cost a tanner," Dad has a light voice, as you'd expect from someone with his physique.

"I'm starving, Joey. Here, I'll get a couple for you."

Dad says no. Why Teazle called him Joey remains – to this day – a mystery. "Teazle" is also a bit of a puzzle. His real name was John Parsons.

They share a corner table quite close to the door. Dad's habit of always giving himself an escape route in life obviously started early. Pubs could be violent, especially with so many soldiers around, and Dad – despite the uniform and everything that went with it – never had much taste for violence.

"What d'you think then, Teaz? You think they'll come? The Germans? Or have we called their bluff?"

Unlike most of the rest of the country, Teazle hasn't given this proposition much thought. The army is three decent meals a day and the promise of foreign travel. He's heard lots about France, chiefly to do with French women and French food. Both sound deeply promising, though he's not sure about the garlic.

"Can't wait," he says. "You think we'll strike lucky?"

Dad laughs. Only this morning he caught Teazle studying a school textbook that included basic French conversation. He's memorised the French for "you're so beautiful", and "will you have a dance with me?", and believes this happy combination will take him through to Paris. Dad, who was hopeless with languages, thinks Teazle's accent is a joke.

"Worth a try though, eh Joey? A bloke in uniform? They won't be able to resist me."

He offers to let Dad come along the first time the regiment gets amongst French girls.

"You can hold my greatcoat, Joey. As long as you promise not to watch."

"You're joking, Teaz. You wouldn't know where to start."

"You don't think so?"

"Never. Those Frenchie women will eat you for breakfast."

The prospect of his two grand passions – food and sex – coming together on a wet night in Northern France does it for Teazle. He empties his glass, and orders another. He gets one for Dad but Dad's had enough so Teazle ends up drinking for both of them. The pub is filling up by now and a bunch of soldiers in the corner have started to sing. Neither Teazle nor Dad know the words, which is just as well because Dad could never sing in tune.

Teazle drinks and drinks. By the end of the evening, in an alley round the corner from the pub, he's being violently ill. Dad, who was always meticulous about detail, notes the curls of undigested onion and somehow gets him back to the regimental quarters where they're all living. The duty sergeant puts Teazle on a charge – drunk and disorderly – and compliments Dad for holding his drink. Three days later, they're all on a ferry heading south.

ABOUT THE AUTHOR

PHILIPPA BOSTON is a writer and journalist who lives in Oxford. As a journalist, she is a columnist and arts writer for the *Oxford Times*. She has published a history of St. Clare's College in Oxford and has extensively studied the city's medieval period. Her short stories have been performed on Radio Oxford, and at the Pegasus Theatre, as well as being published in *The Lady*. She also wrote the title *The Fortunes of John de Courcy* in the Paper Planes Collection. She is a member of Oxford Voices writing group.

The Sorceress
on www.paperplanes.fr:

- the audio version read by Karin Morgan
- Philippa Boston talks about writing *The Sorceress*
- more about English society in the 16th century